GRANDPA'S

OVERALLS

GRANDPA'S OVERALLS

BY

TONY CRUNK

PICTURES BY

SCOTT NASH

ORCHARD BOOKS · NEW YORK

An Imprint of Scholastic Inc.

Orchard Books, an imprint of Scholastic Inc., 95 Madison Avenue, New York, NY 10016

Manufactured in the United States of America
Printed and bound by Phoenix Color Corp. Book design by Scott Nash and Mina Greenstein
The text of this book is set in Soupbone. The illustrations are watercolor.

10 9 8 7 6 5 4 3 2 1

Library of Congress Cataloging-in-Publication Data
Crunk, Tony.
Grandpa's overalls / by Tony Crunk ; with pictures by Scott Nash.
p.   cm.
Summary: When Grandpa's overalls run off, his family and neighbors try to catch them and then pitch in to do
the work that Grandpa cannot do without his pants.
ISBN 0-531-30321-7 (tr. : alk. paper)
[1. Farm life—Fiction. 2. Grandfathers—Fiction. 3. Clothing and dress—Fiction.] I. Nash, Scott, date, ill. II. Title.
PZ7.C88955 Gr 2001 [E]—dc21 00-39942

For my girls—
Maria, Queen, Hanne, and Lady Büüg—T.C.

For my good friend Marc—S.N.

E ARLY ONE MORNING Grandma came downstairs
just in time to see Grandpa's overalls
hop down off their nail on the kitchen wall,
slip out the door, and sneak away across the back porch.

Grandma raised such a ruckus,
it knocked Grandpa, me, and the rest of us
clean out of bed.

Then we ran to the window and—sure enough—
there they went, Grandpa's overalls,
hightailing it past the clothesline
and over the barnyard fence.
"Quick, after 'em!" Grandpa cried.
"I've got work to do today,
and a man can't work in nothin' but his long-handled drawers."

So there <u>we</u> went,
down the stairs and out the door,
across the yard and over the fence—

Grandpa, Grandma, me, and the rest of us—
chasing along behind.

But Grandpa's overalls were nowhere to be seen.
Grandpa was about ready to pop a stitch.
"Never missed a day of work in my life," he said,
"and I ain't about to now."

We heard a commotion from the chicken house
and ran around the barn.
"Come back here, you rapscallions!" Grandpa hollered.
"I've got work to do today!"
He took a flying tackle at them,
but off they ran and disappeared.

Well, by then the neighbors had heard the uproar
and here they all came—
Uncle Eck and Aunt Lou Ann,
Granny Jakes and Old Man Hickum,
Cousin Sadie and Preacher Simms,
the Bunks and their whole passel of little Bunks.

"What's wrong, neighbor?" Mr. Bunk asked.
"My overalls clean ran off," cried Grandpa.
"And I've got work to do today!"
Uncle Eck nodded sympathetically. "A man can't work
in nothin' but his long-handled drawers."

Just then we heard a hubbub from the barn.
Grandpa took off and there we went—
Grandma, me, and the rest of us—
tearing along behind.
And there went Grandpa's overalls . . .

across the garden . . .

into the potato patch . . .

down through the hay . . .

out into the cornfield . . .

and finally up through the apple orchard,
where they took a big leap
high over the treetops.
Off they went, up into the clouds,
swirling and whirling,
clear out of sight.

We just stood there—
Grandpa, Grandma, me, and the rest of us—
shaking our heads,
some of us scratching them,
wondering what would happen next.

Nothing did.

Finally Old Man Hickum said, "Well.
There's a sight you don't see every day."
Which was true.
But poor Grandpa was fit to bust.
"Now what?" he said. "I've got <u>all</u> this work to do,
and here I stand in nothin' but my long-handled drawers!"

But then Granny Jakes rolled up her sleeves,
relit her pipe, and tied down her bonnet.
"Time we all got to work now, isn't it, neighbors?" she said.

So Uncle Eck brought the chickens in,
        and Aunt Lou Ann milked the cow.

Cousin Sadie plowed the field,

and Granny Jakes and Preacher Simms harvested the hay.

Old Man Hickum weeded the garden.

The Bunks and their little Bunks
dug a whole passel of potatoes.

But a man can't work
in nothin' but his long-handled drawers,
so Grandpa spent the whole time sitting
by himself in the smokehouse.
(I peeked in on him once,
and he didn't seem to mind it too bad.)

When the work was all finished,
Grandma called us in: "Suppertime!"

We called Grandpa out on the way to the house
and showed him all the work we had done.
(He didn't seem too disappointed.)

So there we all went, tired but happy—
Grandpa, Grandma, me, and the rest of us—
up the lane and across the yard,
around the house
just in time to see . . .

Grandpa's overalls and Grandma's nightgown
slipping through the kitchen door
and sneaking away across the yard.

"Gracious me!" called Grandma. "A body can't sleep
without her long-tailed nightie. After 'em!"

So there we went—
Grandma, Grandpa, me, and the rest of us—
chasing along behind. . . .